Patrick Crerand

The Paper Life They Lead: Stories

 Arc Pair Press

The stories in this collection originally appeared in the following publications: "PIT-DAY," *New Orleans Review*; "The Glory of Keys," *McSweeney's Quarterly Concern*; "The Paper Life They Lead," *Ninth Letter*; "A Man of Vision," *Conjunctions*; "Semi Love," *Cimarron Review*; "42nd & Lexington," *ekleksographia*; "The Ear," *Masque & Spectacle*.

ISBN-13: 978-1-7339719-2-8

Contents

PIT–DAY

Halfway into the hour flight from Pittsburgh to Dayton, the plane leveled off and the captain made the announcement that they were all flying into outer space. The timbre of his voice was calm as if he were giving a weather report.

"I see a new route marked out for us in the sky," the captain said. "Tiny white clouds shaped like anvils, pointing upward toward the panoply of stars. Below us are the Hopewell Mounds. Those grassy keloids where the gelid remains of a people from a braver age lay. Can you hear them cheering us upward? They're not worried that commuter jets aren't supposed to charge into the upper crust of the atmosphere. They know this plane: its limits and its failures. I can feel it too. Yet I want to do this for all of you: my crewmate, Penelope, sweet Penelope, and my passengers, sweet passengers. I left Flight Officer Brown in the lounge with his cognac, so place your hand over mine on the throttle and we'll etch a new vapor trail of greatness in the sky together. I love you all so very much."

The engines roared and the plane tilted upward. The hollow tube of the cabin erupted into a wash of shrill laughs, but as the passengers felt the weight of the climb and saw the ground grow fainter in the dusky light, a few screams echoed off the hard plastic trays, marking the change in pressure.

In that moment of panic, everyone was an expert on the plane, reciting lines from the safety card as if the complimentary wings on their lapels were real gold and not plastic.

"We'll burn up on re-entry," a businessman in a red repp tie said.

"Forget re-entry," a businessman in a blue repp tie said. "This jet can't break the sound barrier."

Penelope re-wrapped her hair in a bun and told them to stay calm. She tapped on the cockpit door, calmly at first, and then banged her fist in short bursts. Was it their secret knock? Was it Morse code? She felt the passengers wanted the security of knowing without her saying it aloud. She never faced them. The heel of her fist met the door underneath the peephole and the warning sticker that read "Bullet-Proof." In her other hand, she still held the metal ice bucket for the beverage service. The water in the bucket tipped and spilled on the carpet as the plane angled toward the moon.

"Captain," she said. "Captain Graves, let me in. You're upsetting the passengers." She hesitated. "The sweet passengers."

An older man stood up, and from the overhead compartment, found his suede, ten-gallon hat and pulled it down over his square head. He tapped Penelope on the shoulder in a responsible way.

"Step aside, Ma'am," he said.

"We can't break down the door," she said. "It's reinforced."

The man in the ten-gallon hat squinted.

"The only way to Dayton is through that door, Ma'am," he said. "And that there's exactly where we need to go."

The Paper Life They Lead

He made a windup motion with his right leg. The point of his boot glinted silver in her eye as he crouched down low. And then, holding the armrests for balance, he swung his hips up and dropkicked the door in one smooth thrust. The door did not move. After five kicks, not even a dent. The speaker crackled on again.

"Passengers of Flight 1903, there are things a black box cannot tell us: measurements incalculable in the data of the flight recorder. Can these machines mark the memories of this journey, miles above the birthplace of flight? Can they capture the sight of ragged electromagnetic waves spurring from the sun? Or the icy crust evaporating from a comet on its elliptical? There is no air in space to carry these words, so remember them. Deep inside, you ache for the greatness of this journey. It seeps off you in ways you cannot see. It's not long now. We're so close."

Outside the windows, a purple darkness bled through the normal spectrum of sky as they crested into the upper stratosphere. The plane shook violently. Penelope stared open-mouthed at the deep color. From the ground, they must have looked like a star falling all the way across the Ohio sky.

One of the businessmen tugged her arm.

"Hey, you're not in on this, are you?" he asked.

"No," she said. "Of course not."

"You weren't just in awe, were you?" the other businessman asked.

"No," she said. "Not me. I want to go to Dayton. Now no more questions. Put your head in your lap."

"What for?" the businessman asked.

She ignored the question and pleaded with the man in the ten-gallon hat to stop kicking and prepare for the unknown. Her mind raced with the possible and the fantastic: crash landing positions, yellow inflatable ramps, moonwalks, the icy dust of comets, Saturn's rings. But the man kicked on as the engines wheezed for air and the plane reached the apex of its journey. Penelope's legs wobbled with adrenaline and she knelt down to brace herself.

"Hold on," she shouted.

For a moment, she stared at the silver triangle tip of the old man's boot. She felt as if every nerve in her body were pulsing all at once and she would tackle him to the carpet if for no other reason than to stop the constant motion of his kicking. But with the last thrust of the engines, the jittery sensation left her. The plane's nose dipped to the earth. Penelope closed her eyes and felt a strange wetness run up her leg and then noticed for the first time the glittering cube of ice floating in front of her calf. It spun edge over edge, higher into the cabin above her head, past the man in the ten-gallon hat, and finally tapping into the cabin door where it left a trail of water like tiny diamonds. She looked at the man in the ten-gallon hat. One of his legs too now hovered over the carpet. Behind her the passengers were held down by their seat belts, but the spilled ice from the bucket in her hand had gotten loose. Throughout the entire cabin shards of ice were aloft, bedazzled and precessing like slow comets. Then just as quickly as it had arrived, the plane banked with a lurch, and the pull from the turn pushed her and the man in the ten-gallon hat into the door like a sack of stones. The door caved with one last pop and sent them both flying into the back of the pilots' chairs.

The two men in business suits shook her awake. In those first splotchy seconds of consciousness, she watched the man in the ten-gallon hat lift Captain Graves by the shoulders from the cockpit and beat him mercilessly with the safety belt display model.

The Paper Life They Lead

"Wake up!" Captain Graves tried to scream between blows.

Or maybe it was, "Wipe out!"

His voice was too hoarse to be heard clearly. The businessmen stopped tapping her cheek and helped restrain Captain Graves in the jump seat by the door. One of them pulled off his tie—the blue-striped repp—and shoved it in the captain's mouth for good measure. Penelope took a seat near the captain and watched the man in the ten-gallon hat pull the plane out of its bank with ease. She could feel they had returned to a safe altitude. The men in the business suits and the rest of the passengers strapped themselves into their chairs. They didn't stop praying until the intercom dinged.

"Sorry about that folks," the man in the ten-gallon hat said. "Just getting a few last minute tips from the old grounds crew in Dayton. I'm going to go ahead and turn on the fasten seatbelts sign again. We'll be down on the ground in a jiffy. Penelope, please prepare the cabin for arrival."

Penelope gathered ice in a folded napkin for a compress for Captain Graves. She held the wet napkin to his temple. He had managed to spit most of the blue tie from his mouth, but he was still groggy.

"Did we reach the stars?" he mumbled.

"Just sleep," Penelope said.

The landing gear descended and the cockpit door swayed open wildly. From her seat, she caught glimpses of the new captain's grim expression in the green glow of the instrument panel. His tall hat never moved as they made their final approach into Dayton. She could see the new captain had no real love for flying.

The Glory of Keys

On Monday Brian Sullivan did not sleep well, so he sent his Pontiac Sunfire to take his plane-geometry exam for him and never returned to Brookhaven High School. After lunch, Brian's math teacher, Ms. Florida, had to find a new desk for the Sunfire and sharpen its pencil. She opened a window to air out the exhaust, but the kids warmed to the smell of gasoline and oil and overall enjoyed the steady hum of its 2.2-liter Ecotec I4 engine. When Principal Dillard stopped by her classroom at two-fifteen for his daily check— they had been caught canoodling during the Sadie Hawkins dance earlier in the semester—the car was in the back row, with one headlight shining on the purple ink of the dittoed exam.

"Could I have a word, Ms. Florida?" he said.

Ms. Florida stepped out to the hall. The students started to shout the way they would if they were riding a roller coaster. Brian Sullivan's Sunfire honked and flashed its lights so as not to be left out of the hullabaloo.

"How long has there been a car parked in your classroom?" Mr. Dillard asked.

"Just this period," Ms. Florida replied. "But I heard from Mademoiselle Jeanne that it sat in during French class as well."

"Her Intro to French?" he asked.

"No," Ms. Florida replied. "Advanced French."

"Funny," Mr. Dillard said. "That car doesn't seem older than a '98."

"No," Ms. Florida said. "It's a '95. My brother had one just like it, in pearl blue."

Mr. Dillard walked back to his office and rechecked the attendance sheets for the day. Sure enough, in each of Brian Sullivan's classes, the teacher had crossed out his name and written in *'95 Pontiac Sunfire, white with red trim.*

Mr. Dillard thought about calling the Sullivan home, but there had been a surprise locker check that afternoon, and three students had been arrested for felony narcotics. A fourth had been caught with a firearm on school grounds. One of the drug-sniffing dogs had left a trail of runny shit down the halls. The Pontiac Sunfire, Mr. Dillard thought, was a stable vehicle. He recalled a commercial featuring a cherry-red, two-door convertible with a buxom brunette behind the wheel, a woman not unlike Ms. Florida. The commercial's slogan had been *We build excitement.* Ms. Florida's face glowed in his mind. Some things, he thought, were better left as they were.

That first semester, Brian Sullivan's Pontiac Sunfire struggled in the academic arena. Its French accent was a bit throaty, and without the ability to grip a pen properly it had a hard time finishing most of its composition assignments. On the sports field, though, Brian Sullivan's Pontiac Sunfire dominated. In November the football team fitted it with a blue and gold bra, the colors of the Brookhaven Bearcats, and spray-painted a number on each door. Coach Tibbets found himself singling out the car during two-a-day practices for its effort in tackling drills. The greatest insult he could lob at the team became, "You run like a goddamned Corolla."

Against their rival East High, Coach Tibbets strapped chains onto the Sunfire's tires and gave the team a ferocious pep talk that had to be cut short due to the fumes from the car's exhaust. That night, under the klieg lights of Welcome Stadium and the steadicam of the local NBC affiliate, Brian Sullivan's Pontiac Sunfire set a new record for touchdowns in a half (seventeen). It seemed to know exactly where to be to make a play. The senior girls painted its number on their lithe bellies in black shoe polish. A few college scouts were there as well, watching as the Pontiac literally drove circles around East High's elite Tiger defense.

"Do you think it can learn the option?" a scout from Bowling Green State asked.

"Forget it," the man from Ohio State said. He pointed to a smoldering puddle of darkness in the end zone. "We want three yards and a cloud of dust, not ten miles and an oil leak."

But their critical gaze did not inhibit Brian Sullivan's Pontiac Sunfire's good time. At the home-coming dance in the gym later that night, it dee-jayed a blistering set of trance music, opening its doors and blasting its radio until its battery wore down. Coach Tibbets popped the Sunfire's hood to jump it alive again with his Ford Bronco, and all the girls gathered around to watch. Even Ms. Florida stopped making eyes at Mr. Dillard to sneak a glimpse at its greasy block. After two jolts, Brian Sullivan's Pontiac Sunfire sent an arc of light sparking from its battery and set a wall of crepe paper flowers aflame. The girls swooned.

At the after party, Marty Greyerson, the captain of the team and leading receiver, shotgunned beers with the Sunfire in the garage while the rest of the team cheered.

Patrick Crerand

They had set the head of the Bearcat mascot on the Sunfire's hood like a grotesque ornament. A few girls rested on the bumper as it revved its engine. The good times rolled.

As the night wore on, though, the crowd thinned. The other kids roamed the upstairs bedrooms of Marty's house, raiding the liquor cabinet and stealing CDs. They pawed and sucked face. Brian Sullivan's Pontiac Sunfire tried to drive inside the house, too, but Marty's mother had white carpet, and the Sunfire was still dripping green and black blots from the game. Plus someone had jammed a Doors cassette into its deck, and Marty could hear Jim Morrison's mad voice grow louder when the Sunfire rolled closer.

By three, the garage had grown colder. The somber timbre of Jim Morrison echoed off the walls. The Sunfire was deciding whether it felt safe to drive when Betty Heller walked in.

Brian Sullivan's Pontiac Sunfire waited as she walked a slow circle around the edge of the garage. Betty Heller was a nice girl, but with the guys on the team she had a reputation. When she came to the headlights she laid a hand across its hood.

"I feel like..."she said, and paused. "If I could just drive you a bit, maybe. Your paint is so soft." She pressed her left breast against the windshield.

Eventually Betty stroked the wiper until Brian Sullivan's Pontiac Sunfire turned on its emergency flashers and squirted a bit of blue washer fluid on Betty's hand.

"It's okay," Betty said, caressing a dent on its hood. "Leave it there."

There were few corners of Brookhaven High where

The Paper Life They Lead

Brian Sullivan's Pontiac Sunfire did not leave an impression. In Mr. Janney's Physics class, the Sunfire often volunteered for demonstrations, and once let Mr. Janney shoot a potato out of its tailpipe. It tutored Freshman Math in the courtyard before football practice, though most of its pupils struggled to decipher the elaborate system of honks and dings Mr. Ritzenfelter, the enrichment teacher, had laboriously catalogued into a kind of car alphabet. After gym, weaklings without pubic hair took refuge in the Sunfire's trunk when it came time to shower. During Mr. Cappello's Civics course, Brian Sullivan's Pontiac Sunfire led a moment of silence for the victims of an earthquake in Malaysia.

But the sporting arena was its true stage. In the spring, it ran track and threw the shot put. At the district meet, over the protests of the other teams, it took first prize in the hundred-yard dash and ran the mile in just over three minutes. The hurdles proved a bigger challenge, but it placed a respectable fifth, and the *Columbus Dispatch* named it to the All-District team.

So it was no surprise that when votes were counted for the class valedictory speech, Brian Sullivan's Pontiac Sunfire was the overwhelming favorite. Even Betty Heller, who had held a grudge when the Sunfire had stopped returning her calls, could see the logic.

"He's touched so many lives," she told her best friend Carol.

Still, it faced its fair share of detractors. One day, driving to Woodshop, the Pontiac overheard Brookhaven High's guidance counselor, Jerry Whalen, speaking in his office with Principal Dillard. They had just received the results from the Pontiac's employment-aptitude test.

"It says here it should look for a job in the engineering sector," Principal Dillard said. "What's so wrong with that?"

Patrick Crerand

"It leaked a few dots on a Scantron," Mr. Whalen said, "and now we're supposed to believe it's college material? Maybe a Grand Am—but a Sunfire? Its Kelly Blue Book isn't even $2,400, and that's not going anywhere but south. I mean, look, Harry—I'm not in the dream-dashing business, but come on. We'd be better off selling it to East High and buying that new couch for the guidance room."

"It did show promise in Mr. Schneider's art class," Mr. Dillard offered, pointing to the mural of tire tracks on the wall outside. But Mr. Whalen rolled his eyes.

"You'll be the fool of the Principals' Ball, letting it speak at graduation," Mr. Whalen said. "And then who will you come crying to, stinking drunk? You're the one who let this car into everyone's life. Face it, Harry: some cars have it and some don't. Don't build up its hopes that it could be something other than a Pontiac Sunfire."

In the end Mr. Dillard brushed this talk off. During commencement, Brian Sullivan's Pontiac Sunfire walked with the other kids, its tassel secured tightly to its rearview, next to its pine cone–shaped air freshener. It gave a rousing valedictory, according to Mr. Ritzenfelter, who translated it afterward and e-mailed it to the entire district under the subject heading THE GLORY OF KEYS. Principal Dillard taped a Certificate of Attendance onto the Pontiac's back window, and all the teachers signed their name in soap.

Two weeks later, at the Principals' ball, Mr. Dillard danced with his wife while Ms. Florida blinked in his mind like an electric sequin swirling on the disco ball. The other principals called him "VTec" and made childish *vrooms* behind him when he walked to get punch. That night he sat hunched over the telephone in his dark kitchen, speaking in hushed tones to Ms. Florida about how it was her soft shoulders he'd wanted to rest his cheek against. But she had other worries on her mind. She had gotten a flat coming out of the teacher's lot that afternoon and had sat there crying for hours. Instead of changing the tire she had written a note to Principal Dillard's wife. Whenever she felt guilty she did this, he knew; she used it as a way to level them both. The notes were never mailed. With the confession written, she always said, there was no reason to lie anymore.

"I just sat there with grease on me and felt like I would never come clean, Harold," she said.

"About the affair?"

"No," she said. "That car. What kind of world have we sent him out into?"

"The car?" Principal Dillard said. "I don't know. You're just upset. You always get depressed after graduation. But come August it'll be just the same. The excitement will build again. We'll build the excitement together, Jan."

"Stop with the fucking commercials," Ms. Florida said.

In the fall, Brian Sullivan's Pontiac Sunfire enrolled at Ohio State and tried to walk onto the football team, but the campus was enormous and not at all impressed with the fantastic abilities of cars. It wasn't strange to see a microwave cart doing shuttle runs on the lacrosse fields by Lincoln Tower, or to catch the tail end of a juggling performance by the Manda, a double-jointed half-man, half-panda who entertained all comers on the corner of High and 15th. Before the Saturday-morning tailgate at Triangle House, Brian Sullivan's Pontiac Sunfire watched its roommate Charlie and his pledge brothers construct a metallic Holstein that shit stadium mustard and suckled actives with Coors Light from its teats. The Sunfire did a few donuts on the front lawn, but the brothers tired of those antics quickly. When it came time to go to the game, it couldn't fit through the turnstiles at the Horseshoe and ended up giving its ticket away to a scalper.

*

The Sunfire never really felt comfortable among the Buckeyes. It was hard to move around most of the hallways on campus, which had been remodeled in the late sixties based on a narrow, labyrinthine floorplan designed purposely to discourage sit-ins. After a month of frustration, the Pontiac stopped getting its oil changed. One morning it awoke in a pool of its own transmission fluid and Charlie reported it to the RA.

"That leak ruined my DVD player," Charlie testified at the dorm hearing. He held a tartan plaid shirt up for the jury to see. "And I think it's wearing my best polo shirt without asking. That's oil on the collar. I can smell it."

Brian Sullivan's Pontiac Sunfire didn't wait to hear the verdict. After the fall break, it parked in front of the Sullivans' house back in suburban Columbus and didn't return to campus. But Brian Sullivan, who had spent the past year studying to be a peripatetic, had long ago stopped thinking of it as his car. He left its keys on a hook in the kitchen cupboard near the oatmeal and went east to study under a Sufi Mystic in Vermont.

Sometimes the Sunfire took rides past the high school. Once, when it tried to enter the front door, two security guards it didn't recognize demanded to see a visitor's pass. The Sunfire honked for Principal Dillard, but

The Paper Life They Lead

Principal Dillard was no longer there to greet it. It was only Mr. Ritzenfelter, who was passing by on his way to lunch, who averted a greater misunderstanding by explaining that Mr. Dillard had shamed himself and the school by cheating on his wife and had resigned. Now no one could enter the building without a guest pass. The Sunfire backed down the stairs and sat humming in neutral until the security men finally threatened to tow it off school property.

*

In the spring, a reckless cousin of Brian's borrowed the Sunfire one night and drove it to HempFest '02, somewhere near the Buckeye Lake amphitheater, where a huckster convinced him to trade the battery for a bag of low-grade marijuana. The huckster spent the rest of the day selling electrical shocks from the battery to stoners, who jerked and moaned against a background of seamless guitar arpeggios echoing off the smoky hillside. Powerless and distraught, Brian Sullivan's Pontiac Sunfire managed to roll down into the woods near a meth shack. A drifter or two used it as a bathroom, or a place to get high for while. One night a mutt with pups burrowed under the driver's seat and shook through the cold dark hours. Sparrow shit painted its windshield white. The junkies sold the springs from its seats and used the foam to start fires in the rain.

A year passed, and the police raided the meth shack. The city towed the Sunfire back to Columbus and left it in the impound lot under the 315 overpass. It sat parked next to an old Dodge Dart for two months, until it was auctioned to a retired nun who drove it a hundred miles a year, all in the same circuit: from her home to the Kroger to St.

15

Agatha's and back home again. After one trip she left a carton of milk in the trunk for several weeks and the kids in the neighborhood started calling Brian Sullivan's Pontiac Sunfire the "Vomit Comet" because of the musty smell. When they notice it now, it's only to toss rocks at its side or grind their skateboards on its bumper, unaware of that year at Brookhaven when it was king. Such is the fate of cars.

The Paper Life They Lead

1.

Morning on the Pepperidge Farm box is not all chocolate and cheese. The three of them—the farmer, his wife, and the boy—dot the whiteness like breadcrumbs on an apron. It is always cold and it is always morning. When the farmer walks, his feet leave no tracks in the white powder. He is on his way to cut and winnow the tufts of winter wheat that strafe the land below the hill. His hands are small and weak. The wind blows in cold streams and stops him. He scans the horizon and stomps his feet warm. The ache in his knee keeps his leg crooked at a painful angle. It throbs and with each step the ache seeps up his leg and into his groin, then to his heart. He daydreams in the pink reflections the white field leaves on the undersides of his eyes. He can see the day ahead of him: The boy and he will scythe the wheat flat, remove the stalks and then throw the heads in the air, letting the wind take the husks, catching the heads in a basket. They will eat a few to check for blight. The jagged berries will cut up the roof of his mouth if it is a healthy crop. The blood will salt the blandness of the wheat. He can already taste the blood. He limps off again.

17

Patrick Crerand

At dinner, his wife rolls out dough and melts shards of chocolate in copper pots while the farmer eats wheat cakes. His boy, a wiry hand, almost a man, sits next to him. He sleeps in the barn to keep the animals from danger, but the farmer knows there is nothing more dangerous than a lazy hand, so the boy does the morning milking before helping in the field. The boy eyes two white cookies striped with lines of chocolate on the farmer's plate. The farmer lets his mind drift and eats another wheat cake. The bitter scent of cocoa taints the air between them.

"You don't got a sweet tooth, do you?" the farmer says.

The boy looks off through the window where a few Holsteins mingle and swing their udders against piles of chaff near the flour silo.

"Nopet," the boy says, gritting his teeth. "Tooths I got don't taste like nothing."

"Good," the farmer says, looking at the cows.

The boy smacks his mouth as he chews on a brown tobacco leaf.

"That way you ain't got nothing for a wife to spoil cept the rest of you."

His wife raises her brow and spits into the copper pot in her hand. She is a stout woman with thick wrists and tight brown lips. She bakes when he sleeps and fills the huge white ceramic jars in the foil-lined basement with finger snacks: chocolate shortbreads with sugared cheeses, frosted ginger cakes, mint drops, lemon snaps dipped in raspberry jelly. She scrawls the name of a city in black script letters across the belly of each jar. Each city has a story that she tells the boy before he goes to the barn. The farmer does not listen. He allows the boy to eat two cookies after dinner.

"Those are too rich for my stomach," he says after

finishing his wheat cake. "Too much chocolate." He wipes the chocolate from the round face of the white cookies on his plate. They look like dying suns, he thinks.

"Feed them to the cows to sweeten the milk," the boy says, grabbing them.

"Too rich for cow's blood, too," the farmer says.

"The beast doesn't smell the sweet milk," the farmer's wife says. "But he'll smell the stink on you."

As she moves past the boy at the table, a thin veil of flour lifts from her apron and into the air around him.

"No beast I ever seened whoop me," the boy says. "I'm ready for him when he comes."

"No beast I've ever seen at all," the farmer says. "Sweet food like that rots your mind. Turn shadows into nightmares."

"The flour silo's running low," his wife says. She lifts two paper bags full of shortbread and stops near the door to the basement. "You boys rest so you can fill it directly tomorrow," she continues.

A cookie drops from her bag and she eyes the boy before shutting the door. The farmer ignores the look and eats the rest of his wheat cakes in silence.

"Sure is a waste of a cookie," the boy says.

The farmer stares at the orange flame in the seam of the cast iron oven door.

"Just as well if you never ate one."

2.

Morning on the Pepperidge Farm box is a hard light that never lifts. It is as if the farmer's memory is bleached white and hidden deep in the flour silo next to his house. His wife undresses and comes to bed still hot from the basement ovens she had stood over as he slept. He makes room for her, still tired from the day, nuzzling his head into the soft cleft of her underarm, his nose against the side of her white breast.

"Is it time?" he asks.

"We're out of flour," she says.

He pulls her tighter. She sighs and he kisses her ribs.

"It's cold in bed when you're gone," he says. His hand stretches across her hip and runs over the coarse hairs of her thigh. He awakens slowly to her movements.

"I dreamed I heard the boy hollering," he says.

"It was no dream," she says. "He screams in his sleep."

"It's those stories that rot his mind," he says, sitting up. "I want you to stop. It's a paper life we lead here. Nothing more."

"I left something for you on the table," she says.

"My stomach can't take the sweetness," he says.

"Then give it to the boy," she says and rolls her back to him.

"I'll give it to the cows," he says and rises.

Downstairs on the round kitchen table, he finds an oval wheat cake painted in oranges and blues sitting on a napkin with a note addressed to him.

In Milan, the vines wind up steep black hills. The young boys hold onto the green leaves and climb up to pick orange blossoms for the girls who wait below in red velvet dresses. The boys run down the other side and never wipe their chins until the ground flattens.

He opens his eyes fully to the glow of white. The cold

The Paper Life They Lead

cleanses his mind of everything but the morning.

Inside the barn, the farmer helps the boy push the wooden arm to start the turn of the millstone, wearing a deeper groove into the dirt with each pass. Later, the farmer stands on the axis of the wheel and beats out a pace with the leg bones of a cow. The boy sings:

"My legs is stronger than yous legs is stronger than hers legs is stronger than theys legs."

A fine white powder grinds under the stone that the farmer collects into white sacks that he will pour in the silo after dinner.

"How far is it to the edge of our land?" the boy asks, when they rest.

"Far," the farmer says.

"Too far to walk?"

"Far," the farmer says. "No place for a boy."

"Just beasts," the boy says.

"You listen here, boy," the farmer says. "This here's a paper life. Nothing but you, me and your mother. The sooner you see it, the better."

The boy has a hurtful glow in his soft brown eyes that could be mistaken for a pale menace if the corners of his mouth turn up, but they never do. They hang under the weight of his thick lips. The farmer beats the leg bones together and the boy pushes on. Soon a thin line of drool falls from the bottom of his lip and he is singing. He has moldy horse teeth, but he is wiry and limber, the farmer thinks, and he can scythe forty acres of wheat by hand. He'll keep him in this barn for as long as he can, away from his mother, he thinks, which means the boy can spend the whole night dreaming of those white jars in the basement, and the farmer knows that to be a bad thing and almost says that out loud to the boy, but he stops himself and feels the rough edge of the cookie in his pocket. When the boy isn't looking, he licks a bit of mint chocolate frosting toughened by the cold. It is sweet.

After dinner, the farmer rings the bell and the cows file into the barn. He shuts the door behind them and climbs a narrow ladder up into the loft with the two sacks of flour they filled in his right hand. His knee aches as he walks to the door in the corner. The door rattles in its frame from the wind. He can feel the bend in the slats of the wall. Gray light seeps in the space between the joints and marks the path to the roof door where there is a ladder to the top of the flour silo. The light shocks his body and he must wait for his eyes to stop pulsing before he can climb. He takes each rung slowly with the sacks in one hand, thirty rungs, until he can stand on the perch to the silo. When he arrives, he turns and in the distance he can see the black lines on the horizon where they have always been, marking the ends of the box.

His shoulders are just narrow enough to squeeze inside the silo hatch. He empties the white powder into the darkness of the tube and waits there for the cloud to rise up and sting the sight from his eyes. He can feel the warmth of the dank air on his face as if the entire silo is an oven.

Outside the sky is always white, but in the silo, the light cannot reach the deep piles of flour and the farmer stares into the blackness. He licks his finger and draws a line in the dust on the curved wall. Each time his finger retraces the same single line that will be covered in dust when he closes the hatch. The dust tastes nutty and sharp like the ground. He cannot tell how long it has been there. Outside the land is empty and white. The cows in the barn tell him it is not morning. The line on the horizon means the end, he thinks. He sees it there thin and black, like the edge of a blade.

Back in the farmhouse, his legs ache and throb from the climb. When his wife goes to the basement, he walks the boy from the house to the barn. He forks a blanched tuft of dried grass for him to sleep on. A thin layer of chocolate rings the boy's lips. His eyes grow heavy and his legs twitch and shake, too tired to wander off. The farmer pats him on the foot.

3.

Morning on the Pepperidge Farm box bears tragedy. The farmer wakes to a warbling scream coming from the direction of his tiny barn.

"That don't sound like the boy," his wife says.

She nudges one of the farmer's bony shoulders that sit like spades on either side of his head. The scream sounds again. The farmer's body cracks to life as he pulls on his overalls and finds his hat in the closet above his woolen coat.

Outside the wind bends the wheat to the ground and the farmer places the scream on the horizon. It is the boy. He tries to walk faster, but the wind pushes hard against him, and the pain in his knee is searing, so he moves slower until he is over the snowy hill and through the fields. He stares down at the gray stream that flows under the red mill wheel and makes a wiggly wet line across the northern border of his property, petering out into a small pond near a clutch of hemlock trees.

He hears the screech again and sees the boy, shirtless, in the snowy meadow surrounded by the cows, all of them in a circle on the frozen pond.

"What's got into you?" the farmer says. "How'd you get out of the barn?"

The boy's breath puffs around his hair so it looks like his head is slowly melting.

"Lookit," he says and screams again.

"What?" the farmer says. He parts his way through the white silt covering the ground and through the cows to the edge of the pond where he sees a small Holstein calf on the ice. The ice is not thick and the farmer can see the calf's innards peeking out of its ragged anus.

"Lookit," the boy says.

The farmer takes off his woolen coat and places it over the boy's bare shoulders. The boy wrings his hands and looks at the dead calf.

"Ain't no beasts, right," he says.

"She's just dead," the farmer says. He looks down at the boy's feet. He has no shoes on and his toes are dusted white and blue. The farmer tells the boy to follow him back into the house, but he will not move.

"If there ain't no beasts," the boy says, "make it right again."

The boy scrunches his face and widens the base of his legs around the frozen red ground. The farmer knows the strength of the boy's legs and he can't drag him any further than the boy wants to be dragged.

"Please, boy. Let's go in. I promise I'll make it right."

"When?" the boy asks.

"I don't know," the farmer says. "But I promise I will."

The boy looks at the farmer. He can see the corners of the boy's mouth turn up.

"There ain't no beasts," he says.

The Paper Life They Lead

They walk to the house with the wind to their backs. Inside the cabin, the farmer stokes the fire in the oven as his wife heats water in a copper pot. When it warms, she sets it down next to the boy and tells him to put his feet inside. The boy hops next to her and falters every so often on the wooden floor. The color returns to his feet.

"You heard the cow screaming?" the wife asks.

"Yeah," the boy says.

"You didn't see nothing around?"

"Nopet," the boy says.

"Don't go snooping around so this trouble doesn't find you again," the wife says. She goes to the basement and brings back a cookie for the boy: a ginger snap in the shape of a cathedral with four chocolate buttresses and windows of yellow apricot jam.

"When we're going to make it right?" the boy says and looks at the farmer.

"Later," the farmer says.

"In Brussels," the wife says, "the ground is clogged with churches. The women kneel at altars and light candles while the men climb steeples and listen to beasts howl."

The farmer bangs his hand on the table.

"Stop all this," he shouts. "It's a paper life we live here now. There's no beasts on our box. I seen the dark lines on its edges. I'll show you the lines and the other side where there ain't nothing and we'll throw that calf over the edge. There ain't no beast, just those lines. That's it. Now, I have chores to do and I'm going to do them. When you feel better boy, you better be out there to help me work them fields."

"What about the calf?" the boy asks.

"He ain't going nowhere," the farmer says. "We'll make it right later. Chores first."

"When?" the boy asks.

Patrick Crerand

"Tomorrow," the wife says. "You make it right tomorrow."

The farmer slams the door behind him and stares out into the hard light. The wind dries his eyes as he walks. Near the barn he finds three more sacks of flour and carries them to the top of the silo. He tries to keep the bags even with his waist as he climbs, but with each rung he feels them sink lower until he can no longer lift them. The burlap slips from his sweaty palms and he watches a bag fall to the roof and spill out in a cloud of white that a gust quickly scatters. He puts his arm through the rung and waits to regain his strength and holds onto a sack with his teeth. Three is too many, he thinks. He can feel the bag slipping from his teeth. The wind pushes against the sack in his left hand and his body lists with it. He opens his mouth and the other sack falls below his feet. He does not see it hit the roof. He looks up at the perch. Ten more rungs, he thinks, and climbs to the top.

Inside the dark silo, he spills out the remaining bag and a fine crust of flour covers his eyes so that he cannot see the edges on the horizon when he emerges. He has never had the strength to reach the lines from the ground, but in his dreams he has traced them with his footsteps and peered into the blankness beyond the edge bravely. They are there, he thinks. Lines mean the end of things. And any dead thing must be thrown over that edge. But he can feel the heaviness in his legs and arms from the day. He cannot remember if it is time to make the line on the rounded wall of the silo, but he traces it over again with his finger anyway.

"Tomorrow," the farmer says.

4.

Morning on the Pepperidge Farm box never ends. There is no night. The whiteness seizes the black from the sky, covers it in an ashen crispness. He awakens to his wife standing over him. Her hands are blackened with soot. He sits up in bed and asks what is wrong. He can see now the flecks of red and white on her apron.

"Is it time?" he asks.

"You have to bury the calf."

"I have chores," he says.

"They'll wait," she says. "The boy is moaning again. I told him to come down and rest."

"Leave the boy," he says. "Let me get you more flour first then we'll take the calf."

He sits up and listens to her walk back down to the basement. He hears the soft moan of the boy echo up the walls. He does not dress. He follows her down into the kitchen and opens the door by the oven. The basement is dark and hot from the cookies that sit in the white ceramic pots along the wall covered in tin foil.

He can see the white rectangular biscuits covering the entire floor. The red log cabin and the white silo, each with colored icing spread in short knife strokes, stand in the middle. A dusting of flour sits on top of each bar like snow extending all the way to the walls, as long and wide as three men. The glow of the white cookies shines horribly on the foil walls. The boy kneels in the middle of the whiteness, crying.

"On the Pepperidge Farm," the wife says, "the white fields are made of flour and not snow. The women bake the cookies and fill white jars in the basement lined with silver foil and a beast stalks a land without edges, searching for farmers and their paper lives. There are no boys on the Pepperidge Farm, only beasts."

The farmer looks into the reflection of the foil and sees the whiteness of the flour climb the walls. He cannot see the lines of his box. The whiteness extends endlessly and makes him dizzy. He grabs the boy and pushes him up the stairs.

"The boy and I are going to hurl that calf over the edge of this box," he says. He feels as if he is outside, as if the wind is blowing so fiercely, he can hardly suck in a breath. "When I return, I want this all gone. It's a paper life here and there's no place for any of this."

The farmer staggers up the stairs and pushes the boy ahead of him. He finds his overalls and boots and calms the boy. "There are no beasts," he says. "Go to the barn. Get the rope and the axe."

The boy does as he is told and when he returns, he is calmer and they walk out to the pond together, step for step at first, but then the farmer feels the tightness in his thighs and starts to lag behind. Past the red water mill wheel, he leans on the boy's shoulder and uses the axe as a cane until they reach the edge of the pond. The calf has frozen to the surface. The farmer is still panting when the boy chops into the sliver of ice closest to the white skin of the calf. It loosens quickly and the boy pulls a big chunk out and ties a rope under the hind legs.

"Heave it," the farmer says and they do. With each pull, the farmer can feel his legs throb and ache. The rope turns in his hands and squeezes his fingers numb. The calf's body slides onto the white ground.

"Where we now?" the boy asks.

The Paper Life They Lead

The farmer can hear the crack in his voice. "We'll throw it over the edge," he says, pointing to the horizon.

The farmer searches for the dark lines, but he can only see a white cloud of snow blowing around him. "Keep on," he says and walks while the boy pulls ahead with the calf.

They pull through the cluster of hemlocks until the farmer can no longer see the pond in the distance behind him. The land is flat and the hard light shines all around them. The wind wipes their tracks clean.

"I might can see from the top of the silo," the boy says, "to sees how far to them lines."

But the farmer shakes his head.

"Pull," he says.

The farmer and the boy drag the carcass further. Behind the fields the farmer cannot see the white tower of the silo. He knows the boy has never been to the top of the silo, but he has watched the farmer and knows the ladders. The calf is so heavy. Its tongue is frozen, its insides are shredded and gray. The rope hurts his hand. He knows the lines aren't much further, so he looks up every few steps for the black lines to appear, but his eyes cannot blink away the glare of the whiteness. His knee locks and wobbles. He can hear the rope crackle from the cold. He tells the boy to pull on while he rests and stretches his legs. A cloud of snow and vapor envelops him as he rests.

"You keep on, boy. I catch up."

The boy nods. The farmer closes his eyes and holds his hand to his face. He finds relief in the darkness, until he can no longer hear the ice crackling under the weight of the calf's body and the footfalls of the boy. He opens his eyes and scans the horizon again. The boy's voice is distant. He wonders how long he has rested. The sky is so white. He counts the beats of his heart drumming in his head.

"Is we headed right?" the boy asks.

His voice is slow and distant.

"Look for the lines," the farmer shouts. "They out there."

He feels breathless. The boy's voice is on the edge of his hearing.

"All I sees is white," the boy says.

"No," the farmer says, placing a hand on his chest as if to contain its heaving. "You ain't looking hard enough." The farmer listens with his whole body, leaning toward the hills and the white empty fields around him, but he can no longer see the horizon. The wind dampens the boy's voice into a whimper. The farmer's pulse rushes in his ears.

"I walk to you," the farmer says, but it hardly travels out of his mouth before the wind blows it back toward him. He strains to listen above his pulse and kneels to catch his breath. The steady pattern of his heart sounds like approaching footfalls of the boy, and the farmer is relieved for a moment until he hears the boy's voice again so far from him. The white cloud drifts so slowly in front of him. He could wipe it with his hands. The boy has pulled too far, he thinks. The boy has fallen over the edge.

"Boy," the farmer shouts. He holds his heart and the footfalls of his pulse slow until finally the boy's voice arrives clearly.

"I sees it!" the boy shouts. "I sees the beast!"

The boy is running to him. The wind carries a putrid smell and the boy emerges from the whiteness and tries to help the farmer to his feet, but the farmer cannot stand. He can only kneel and moan softly, pawing at the boy's clothes to keep him near.

The Paper Life They Lead

"Stay with me, boy," he says.

But the boy is running fast now toward the silo, looking back now and again at him. His legs are strong enough, the farmer hopes, never to see what is coming behind him. With his last bit of strength, the farmer reaches out to the darkness that gathers near him and holds out his finger as if to touch it, as if to taste its sweetness.

A Man of Vision

for Richard Connell

Late in the afternoon, the donors and their children toured the old abandoned zoo pavilion. Their guide, a man dressed in khaki, walked at the front of the group, noting points of interest along the dirt path before finally stopping near a railing that stood above an enormous gravel lot deep inside the maze of moribund paddocks and halls. The lot itself held no animals, only the odd plastic bag and Styrofoam cup. A sharp smell of decay festered in the air heated by the last rays of that day's sun. They were relieved to stop, but the man in khaki did not seem to be sweating. He wore a set of field glasses around his neck and carried a rifle by its fluted end like a walking stick. He pointed at the lot behind them and spoke of the dismal status of the zoo's predators. Though his tone had been dour for most of the tour, the donors appreciated the affected spirit of his accessories, which he wore especially, in their opinion, for the sake of the children. Several times during his tour, he had crouched down to their level and pointed out the tracks of animals preserved in cement on the zoo walls or allowed them to use his field glasses to spy a stray bird scavenging the bare floor of an old paddock. He was a good sport, this man in khaki, they all agreed.

"Imagine," the man in khaki said, gathering the

children near him, "the dangerous rivulets of the Serengeti meeting the treacherous sloughs of a Brazilian rain forest *and* the forbidden tundra of the Arctic. Imagine lions, hyenas, tigers, jaguars, anacondas, and polar bears, all in one space, all in *this* space. The greatest predators of the world lurking around every inch of dirt, mud, and ice for your viewing pleasure. It's all possible with just a few donations."

Some of the donors jockeyed with the children for better views of the empty gravel lot in the low light of the afternoon, pushing the man in khaki closer to the railing so that the fluted end of the rifle barrel clanged against the steel bars like the chimes of some distant clock.

"Below us," the man in khaki continued, "picture a watering hole complete with sandstone rocks and a swaying palm tree or two. The stream will be fed by a larger pool, fifty feet deep. Next to it, a frozen tundra where we can ship in mounds of snow and ice completely refrigerated. To the right, brown vines and creepers will hang below and tangle with giant milk tree leaves of the Amazonian jungle. We'll have rain sprinklers, real lava slides, a snow machine running every day."

The donors gleamed and pressed closer to the bars. As they listened, they inched the children out of the way, apart from a few bolder preteens who had climbed up the fences and sat on the top railing.

"Of course," the man in khaki continued, "all of this will be written down on several large bronze plaques to explain how these predators have no other place to go and how the world is bent on their extinction, et cetera, et cetera." He pointed to the black steel bars of the railing and with his other hand outlined the rectangular shape and the size of the plaque much to the donors delight. "And then," he continued, "a bas relief of the face of the greatest donor emblazoned here on a separate plaque. It will read, 'Our eternal gratitude to that most generous benefactor who manufactured a habitat out of the good will of his or her heart.' Again the wording is open to negotiation."

The donors could almost see their names in bronze, and the group broke into applause. The man in khaki stood and held the rifle over his head like a T to gain their attention. "But before this vision can be realized, we need your help. There can be no mission without money. Shall we open the bidding for the first plaque at five thousand?"

"Five thousand," a man in a navy blazer shouted.

"Seven," another screamed.

"Seven five," still yet another man yelled.

The man in khaki strained to keep up with the figures being shouted, but then his voice settled in the low, bumpy tone of an auctioneer. He sold the first plaque in ten seconds, slamming his fist into the palm of his other hand to complete the sale. The largest plaque with the bas relief took longer, but the man in khaki pointed each bidder out clearly, stabbing his finger in the air to each man, woman, or child who spoke.

During the exclamation of bids, it was apparent two separate groups had formed. With each shout and mad gesture of the first group, the members of the second moved to the back, allowing the most fervent to form a semi-circle around the man in khaki. The women of this closest group shrieked and elbowed, flashing their diamond brooches and gaudy baubles as their husbands in new tuxedoes postured and rolled up their sleeves, digging in for a fight. But the man in khaki, it seemed, never lost sight of the second group behind the loudest bidders.

This group was made up of more reserved members,

and they bided their time in the back, knowing well that such noise was the behavior of junior executives, the men and women who worked on the floor of the exchange rather than those who ran it from private office suites up above. Among this second group of bidders was a large woman who wore a black dress patterned with white and yellow orchids that lolled obscenely around her rotund figure. Somehow the small child in her arms remained asleep amidst all the shouting. The boy wore a gleaming white suit with gold piping around the hems and looked like a midget admiral.

While the first group exhausted themselves haggling over the wording of the plaque, the man in khaki stepped away and walked forward up the path to a brick ledge overlooking a piece of empty grassland, two football fields wide. The area was surrounded by an enormous fiberglass rock wall and below the wall, a moss-filled moat. A few lines of thick wild bushes grew greenly in the middle. The rotund woman walked to the front of this second group and nodded at the man in khaki upon her arrival. He returned her nod with a cavalier wink that seemed to convey a hidden predatory knowledge of the business world. The man in khaki gathered the second group by the ledge.

"Pray tell, sir," the woman asked, peering over the bricks, "what plans do you have for this space here?"

The group of junior executives gestured for order, clearing their throats in authoritative fashions, but the man in khaki turned his attention to the large woman and her cadre.

"Madame," the man in khaki said, "you have quite an eye. My compliments. You have found my favorite paddock of the old zoo. It is one of the few exhibits that we maintained while the others went abandoned."

The man in khaki stood up on the ledge and leaned

over, pointing his gun toward the dense brush in the lower right corner of the grassland, just above the low moat that ran along the bottom edge of the property. The area he spoke of fell nearly behind them, so close to the ledge they stood upon that the group could see only the tips of the green shoots and barbs stretching out over the moat. The man in khaki invited them all up on the ledge to get a closer view. The first group had brushed off the indignity of the man in khaki's absence like pocket lint and now crammed in tighter around the ledge with the others, so as not to miss an opportunity to compare their lot with the paddock below them.

"Somewhere deep in that brush," the man in khaki said, "rests one of the greatest predators ever to stalk the earth, the giant seven-toed sloth."

A baronet in a navy blazer from the first group coughed out a crude laugh. "A sloth?" he asked. "I see an empty field," the baronet shouted. The baronet's blazer had a crest embroidered on his breast pocket in garish reds and blues that perhaps represented his last thread of nobility, but the bald man's leathery face seemed more fit for attending a yacht than owning one. The first group, hoping to impress him, broke into a curious laughter, but the people on the ledge leaned closer to catch a view.

The man in khaki remained stony-eyed. "The giant seven-toed sloth is one of the few predators on earth to survive throughout the previous five eras of extinction, sir. I shouldn't have to tell you, sir, that its lone defense all this time has been its impressive camouflage. I shouldn't have to tell you, sir, that a cursory glance into the brush wouldn't be sufficient to see it. I should think, sir, you should expect more from such a predacious beast than to reveal itself on the whim of some mortal," he hesitated. "Baronet, is it?"

Patrick Crerand

The baronet looked down at his oxblood loafers and scuffed the ground. "Please continue," he said. "I humbly apologize."

The man in khaki resumed his position facing the group on the ledge, holding the barrel of his rifle against his leg. "As I was saying, the sloth has survived ice ages, catastrophic meteorite impacts, volcanic eruptions, super typhoons, tsunamis, and earthquakes immeasurable on the Richter scale. Its reign stretches from the era of the dinosaurs to modern times. It has lived on every continent and on top of every food chain. From the earliest days of this present era, men have burned it, speared it, clubbed it, shot it, hanged it, and recently attempted to obliterate it with weapons of mass destruction. Its metabolism is so slow, its will so relentless, however, that nothing can kill it."

"Nothing?" the baronet asked.

The man in khaki turned to eye the first group behind him. "Oh, I *could* pump it full of lead, as the saying goes, but it would still take an eon to die, and before it did, the giant seven-toed sloth would eventually hunt me down and eat me. You see, it not only survived the five eras of extinction, but this seven-toed species is responsible for the extinctions of most of the mammals, birds, and insects that have vanished from the planet thus far. Even our dear director, after he found this one in a South American rainforest, had to give his own life to keep it in this zoo."

The man in khaki stepped up onto the ledge and gathered some of the children around him. "As you can see, this paddock requires a sizeable endowment and a terrific commitment to maintain and preserve this most dangerous of species. Who among you can help contain its poisonous musk from leaking out into the megacities and infecting hundreds of millions? Who can sate its need for the millions

38

of blood tulips it requires not to grow wearisome during its captivity? Who will pay for the tarantula webbing flecked with gold dust above its fountains of mercury that it has come to appreciate? Can we put a price on the enjoyment of future generations of such a treasure as this sloth? Surely you don't expect me to come up with a bid?"

The man in khaki paused and listened to the members of the first group protest for, at the least, a guiding value. But the man in khaki stepped down among them and turned his back to face the group on the ledge. The rotund woman quickly silenced their meek bickering.

"Three million dollars," the rotund woman said. She set her son down on the ledge next to her and shot a fierce look down the line at the remaining bidders standing on the ledge with her. She eyed each man and woman carefully and one by one they stepped down until only the rotund woman, her child, and a man with a black eye patch stood.

"Three million five," the one-eyed man said.

"Four," the rotund woman countered. "And I want my name in gilded letters on a wrought iron archway above the whole pavilion."

"Five million!" the one-eyed man countered.

"Six!" the rotund woman said.

The bidding rose steadily. The man in khaki never spoke but stabbed wildly in the air like a conductor at a symphony. The rotund woman was savvy though. After the last bid she curled her finger and called the man in khaki over to her, resting her ample bosom on his shoulder. "How much for the whole she-bang?"

The man in khaki whispered in her ear and the woman licked her lips and threw up her hands with joy.

"I'm in for it all!" she shouted. Before the man with the eye patch could speak, the man in khaki slammed the butt of the rifle against the ground.

"Sold!" he said.

The rotund woman was elated. The flowers on her dress writhed as she danced on the ledge, lost in the joy of owning what even the most privileged could not own, but in her excitement she forgot that her son was next to her and, with one careless jolt of her hips, knocked the boy off balance. He teetered on the corner of the bricks for a moment waving his arms and smiling, before falling awkwardly off the ledge. The donors gasped as the boy flipped several times and landed with a splash thirty feet below them in the green water of the moat. The rotund woman screamed. From their vantage, the crowd could see the boy's fleshy expression tighten his eyes into slits. But before he could let out a wet cry, his mother pointed at the grass and let loose a terrific yelp:

"God in heaven, the sloth, child! Run for the rocks."

"No!" the man in khaki screamed. "Stop where you are, boy!"

At first the child looked stupidly and blankly at the crowd, but his mother had screamed so loudly that he had no choice but to ignore the unfamiliar yell of the man in khaki and run. The donors followed the boy as he dashed out of the water and up into the field.

"Stop running!" the man in khaki shouted again. "It's the worst thing you can do! Stop! Stop!"

This time the boy listened. He stood wide-eyed on the grass.

"We're coming," the rotund woman said. She looked at the crowd below her and the man in khaki. "Save him," the rotund woman pleaded. "Please save my boy!"

"I'm afraid I cannot," the man in khaki said.

The Paper Life They Lead

"Nonsense," the baronet said. He stripped off his jacket and rolled up his pant legs. "Surely there's a ladder. It can't be more than twenty feet. I'll jump down and the boy can climb up with me."

"No," the man in khaki said. "Once the sloth has smelled the boy, it's only a matter of time." He peered through the field glasses and pursed his lips, and then looked at his watch. In the western horizon, the sun was a wavering globule of orange light.

The baronet put his oxblood loafer on the angled edge and knocked a dusting of mortar off with the sole as if to prepare to jump the gap, but the man in khaki pulled him back with the butt of his rifle. He pointed the gun at the baronet and corralled him into the larger group of donors.

"You don't know what you're dealing with," the man in khaki said. He wrapped the strap of his rifle around his forearm to steady his aim.

"It's a damned sloth!" the baronet said.

"No one is moving an inch," the man in khaki said.

The boy continued to cry out for his mother below them. A sickly patch of yellow stained the front of his white trousers. Still the man in khaki did not lower the barrel of his rifle from the middle of the group.

"You can't shoot us all," the baronet said.

"No," the man in khaki said, "but if I did, it would be a more civilized death than what would happen should you end up down there with that sloth. It hunts at night. Its movements are slow, but it never stops. Humans need sleep and rest, but the sloth never does. It lives on one meal every 280 years if necessary. Once it smells you, it can move faster, but death for the victim is inevitable and quite slow. It has no incisors, only rough molars, so it can't cut through you as much as it has to gnaw. There are reports of one eating a man for ten long years. Think of it, ten years of being chewed on. Of gaining strength to run more only to fall again and be chewed on more, until the day, when you can't run any longer. This sloth here sniffed our own dear departed director as an infant in Peru. He and his parents were disembarking from a ship on the coast. Thirty years later, it finally began eating when he passed out in an alley in Montevideo. It tracked him all the way across two continents, where it finished the job not far from where the boy stands now."

The rotund woman screamed again and this time stepped down from the ledge limply and then collapsed onto the dusty ground with a hard thump. A few of the sturdier men laid her out. The baronet rolled his navy blazer into a pillow. He stood over her and smacked her face until she returned to consciousness. A splotchy rash marked the places where the boy had grabbed her arms just minutes earlier.

The rotund woman came to. She still had the boy's white cap in her hand and she clutched it as she staggered to her feet. "Blessed mother, run to the rocks, son!"

The boy ran in a long curve away from the bushes and the ledge, as if one leg were shorter than the other.

"He'll only make himself look more like prey," the man in khaki said. "Stop!"

"Zig, now zag," the man with one eye offered.

The man in khaki swore and raised the rifle and fired a single shot into the air. It echoed above the pavilion and out into the pink light of the western sky.

"The sloth abhors confrontation, boy!" the man in khaki said. "Your only chance for survival is to stand your ground."

The small white figure stopped in his tracks as if he

had been shot. The sun had dipped low nearly behind the wall now. The grass was coated in jagged shadows. After a long pause, the rotund woman spoke.

"How long must he stand there?" she asked.

"I'm afraid," the man in khaki said, "for the rest of his life."

"Let me go in," she pleaded, inching nearer to the man in khaki. "Let me take his place. Give me the gun. I'll shoot it dead."

"If you shoot it," the man in khaki replied, "you'll only make it madder. It's been on the earth for millennia. Think of the rage it has stored up over that period of time."

"Surely one body is as good as another though. Let me go in."

"It's too late now," the man in khaki replied. "The sloth has already smelled him. If you went down now, he would eat both of you eventually."

"Shoot it, you coward," the baronet shouted.

"And waste a perfectly good sloth?" the man in khaki said. "My dear baronet, you reveal your true self. Why kill the sloth? After all, isn't it just doing its job? Isn't this why people come to a zoo: to see a predator in its natural element? As a zoo conservationist, I don't think I need to explain to you about the endangered status of these sloths or how hard they are to come by. No, as long as the boy stays in the paddock, the sloth will not harm him or any of us. It will be fed and survive for future generations to enjoy."

In the paddock, the boy stared at the line of bushes and then turned to face the crowd. He cried out to his mother. He was no bigger than a thumb now, a white blob far away from all of them.

"Please," she cried. "The boy can climb out himself. He could have a fruitful life before it found him. I'd put him far away at sea or in a rocket orbiting the earth. The sloth could never find him there. I'll pay you any amount of money. Whatever you want, it's yours. Just give me back my boy. He could still have a fruitful life. Please! I beg of you."

The man in khaki paused and fingered the nipple of his gun. The line of his mouth tilted diagonally. "It's possible the boy could outrun the sloth, but it's very doubtful. This sloth will surely outlive every last one of us gathered here. But my concern is what would the boy's life be like if he climbed out of the paddock?"

"It could still be good," the mother said. "I'd make sure of it."

"No," the man in khaki said. "I think it would be dreadful. For the rest of his life, every moment, every great accomplishment, and every great joy would be tempered by the unbearable pain of knowing the horrible death that awaited him. As a humane man, I couldn't free the boy and live with myself afterward knowing that that would be his future. It may be hard to realize, but this is for the best."

The woman stared at the man in khaki and her face loosened for a moment as if she recognized him from some dinner party held long ago. Behind him in the grass, she could see the last spots of sun touch the brush. The boy cried out still.

"Think of how much less you'll worry," the man in khaki said. "You'll never have to wonder is my boy in danger or will he come back from school today. All those sleepless nights wondering if he'll be a genius or a dunce, if he'll be a failure or fall just short of the success you've attained. It's all settled here and now."

The man in khaki lowered his rifle and led the crowd back to the front entrance of the zoo, leaving the mother alone on the brick ledge. In the parking lot, they waited for the valets to bring their vehicles. The women winced from each of the boy's screams while the men made small talk to cover the noise. Better to put it right out of your mind, they told their wives. When the baronet's vehicle arrived, he paused and put a hand on the man in khaki's shoulder and nodded. Before each of them drove off, it seemed, every one of the donors had touched him on the shoulder or taken his hand in theirs and spoke of the kindness and the rigid constitution such a situation dictated, all except the mother, who remained on the ledge, staring down at the boy until the darkness came fully and neither could see the other.

Semi Love

"I'm leaving at first snow," Georgia said to me one day. This was back when all I had was my stink and the love of a woman who wore neon.

"My sweet Georgia, you'll never leave," I said.

We were sitting on deck chairs in the grass. The sun was fading down into the soft green hills stretched out on the horizon like moldy bosoms. I was watching the birds feed and playing tin whistle ditties for them. She drank milk from the carton. I told her we had a complex relationship based on temporary lapses in repulsion. I told her she'd change her mind.

She stared off at her broken down rig parked next to the warren of sectional houses I managed. The truck was powder blue with a twenty-seven inch TV in the back she covered up with a Confederate flag, which she said was a joke. My people were from the same town in Ohio as Sherman. We met at a rest stop diner off I-55 a few years earlier. I was transporting temporary homes, an oversized load on the *via dolorosa*. She was the child of a missionary but found her calling driving trucks full of cows up and down the country. We courted via CB. Now we were both exiled in the Wisconsin Dells with only the occasional acorn dropping on our roof to distract us from life.

"I've got a bird that whistles," I sang. *"Life don't mean a thing."*

"I'm going to make you swallow that whistle if you don't stop," Georgia said.

I stopped and watched dusty yellow flecks of seed spurt out the holes I'd made in a two-liter of soda that hung from my roof.

"Did you even hear me?" she asked.

"You'll come around again," I said. "You won't go."

More birds chirped at my feet, so she threw a rock at the group of them. The faster birds dodged the rock she threw, but one bird was too fat to move. It was black and lumpy and could hardly stand. It tried to eat the rock that Georgia had thrown and then waddled closer to my feet to rest. It was the fattest bird I had ever seen.

Georgia threw another rock over and nearly hit the fat bird again.

"Stop now," I said. "It can't hardly fly."

I scooted the bird away from her with my foot. It pecked at the ground, then lolled on its side panting, not chirping. The bird had a red puff of feathers on each wing and breathed hard as it bounced. It never once took flight. I said I thought it was an oriole.

"That's no oriole," Georgia said.

She was some kind of dream killer.

*

Georgia had a keen sense of direction. We once took a walk in a forest of hemlocks that surrounded a lake. From above, the lake looked like a giant peanut. She ran ahead and left me in that forest. Night was close, and I was drunk with fear. She kept walking around and around until she found her way deep into a clearing using nothing but her crooked nose. When I found her, she was sitting on a rock near the water. Her skin was flushed and glowing white, and her dark hair smeared across her forehead. It was like she'd been reborn. She made room for me on the flat edge of the rock. She spoke of the cows.

"Before the drive," she said. "I'll pull over to the side of the road near a grazing field. You can tell if it's going to rain because they'll be out under a tree like a clump of mushrooms hours before a cloud is in the sky. But they know. When I walk over to the fence, they stand up and those sharp shoulder bones stretch their skin like wet paper. They walk out to see who I am. They're so stupid. They should run away and hide. 'I'm the one who drives you to the butcher,' I say, but they're drawn to movement and don't know better. They eat anything if it's in the grass. Nails, barbed wire, tires. They make the cows swallow a magnet when they're young to collect all the metal they eat in their first stomach, before it tears up the rest of their insides. When they're close enough to touch, I can see it's not paper at all that hangs down on their bones. If they just stayed under that tree, no one could move them. The smaller ones could crush me, but even the adults climb up into my truck easy every time. I pray for them all when I drive. I pray, 'God, let me see the world with eyes that innocent.' I pray, 'Tell me where to go.'"

She held the rough edge of her hand in mine. We stayed on that rock for another hour or so shivering and then I looked at her like I wanted to leave and she kissed me for the first time. I kissed her back, and we sat there on that cold rock kissing for an hour until I was sweaty and nervous that maybe all this kissing was Georgia's way of hiding that she was just as lost as I was, and so I stopped kissing her for a moment and I leaned in close to her ear and whispered, "Just where do you think we are exactly?" And I thought she would just whisper back a response, hot and breathy, in my ear, but she pulled me right up and led me by the arm out of the woods instead.

It's clear to me now that we were in the forest of hemlocks, on the lake that from above was shaped like a giant peanut.

*

Weeks passed and the snow formed a hard crust around the sectional homes, but Georgia stayed and the bird came inside. I named it Abel and slept with him in the bed to keep warm. He was like a hot water bottle with wings. Once I fed him too many sunflower seeds and crackers and whatever else I couldn't eat from dinner.

"Birds shouldn't eat instant potatoes," Georgia said.

I wanted to tell her that Abel only ate the tan gravy that covered the potatoes, that the plumage of some orioles had been known to thrive on it, according to some experts, but I was never one to pick fights.

"He needs to migrate," I told her. I drew Abel a bath in a roasting pan. The water made the patches of red on his wings glow. "Maybe we'd take him down south?"

"We," she repeated. She had a way of talking under her breath like she was still on the CB with miles of static flowing between us.

"Maybe?" I said again.

But she walked away and sat in the cab of the semi for a little while and listened to the real chatter on the CB

The Paper Life They Lead

until it was dark.

"We drink from the same dish now," I said to Abel.

We slept that night on newspapers under the only southerly exposed window. When I woke, Georgia read the classifieds tattooed backwards on my cheek. She called me a fool and kissed me on the forehead.

By the time the mechanic got around to fixing the engine to her rig, the ground had frozen and the bird no longer had a neck.

*

I woke up on one of those days where you couldn't tell if the sun was slowly rising or slowly falling. Georgia was packing. She came into the room with her bag in her hand and looked at the bird on the floor. He waddled over to her and she picked him up.

"We'd like to go with you," I said.

She stared at me like she was lost.

"Just the bird," she said and walked out the door.

The engine rattled the walls of my house. I followed her outside. My breath and the exhaust from the truck mingled above me and hovered over the white expanse of land.

"Where are you going?" I asked.

"South enough for him," she said.

"For how long?" I asked.

The trees around the trailer park were empty and covered with ice. She had the two-liter bird feeder from the roof in the cab already.

"You'll find me again," she said.

Just then I tried to grab her. I wanted to see my hand print in red in her arm, but I couldn't move. I could feel it there in my gut, like I had swallowed a magnet too, and it was turned the wrong way from hers, pushing me softly away.

42nd & Lexington

I felt she was a symbol of the city less so because I met her in midtown and more so because her breasts were skyscrapers. Both of them, shapely and rounded when under her silk blouse, expanded into exact replicas of the Chrysler Building when she took off her bra. She was the first woman I had ever loved with art deco nipples. Her name was Toby. We went back to her loft after drinks. I undressed under a girder. She called me closer to her bed by a giant window with chicken wire glass. There she revealed them to me. Normally I was a gentleman, but I had had a lonely childhood marked by bullies and model planes. I didn't even look her in the eye. Not even a kiss. My hands cupped under the long brick tier of the building, rubbing back and forth between the silver statue of wings and up toward the iron eagle heads that guarded the corners below the stainless crown.

"Don't squeeze so hard," she said, pushing me onto the bed. "You'll break the lights on the viewing gallery."

"Sorry," I said. I rubbed the antennae between my thumb and forefinger. "Is this steel?"

"Yes," she said, rolling her eyes.

"How did they—"

She planted her hand on my chest and dug in with her nails.

"They don't even smell like glue," I said.

"Are we going to do this or what?" she asked, yanking my chest hair.

"Yes," I said. "Yes!"

A few of the workers in the offices around the 39th floor had opened their windows to watch. I could hear them making catcalls.

"You can do better, Toby."

"His ass is dented like his face!"

"Touch her where she pees!"

I was having a hard time performing in front of the crowd, but Toby pulled me toward her chest and moaned and the hard brick edges of the towers scraped my face raw. The pain sharpened me until I was throbbing. Still I had so many questions.

"I didn't think those windows could open," I said as she ground her hips into mine. "The hinges must be incredibly nimble. And the workers? What do you charge for rent?"

"I'm trying to get off," Toby said. "Get with it or get out."

She rocked her hips harder and I sat silently transfixed by the lines of small lights, those tiny chevrons stacked one atop the other, and for a moment, with my hand alongside hers on the side of the building, I thought I could feel the rumble of the elevators.

"Van Alen!" Toby shouted.

"My name isn't—" But she put a finger on my mouth and arched her back.

"Don't you even move," she said.

*

The Paper Life They Lead

Toby slept with her back to me. The soft glow of the tiny office lights cast pale squares onto the chicken wire. It looked like a glass checkerboard, and I played a game in my head, kinging myself, until Toby rolled over and the board blackened. As if on cue, a stream of men and women, each no taller than a pen's nib, piled through the banks of revolving doors by her cleavage. They slid down the notches of her ribcage, carrying leather valises, umbrellas and messenger satchels, and then walked into the darkness, toward some unknown corner of the loft, toward some mean life in an undisturbed borough behind the glass checkerboard. One of them, a man with bronze skin, came up to my pillow and spoke in my ear. He carried a bucket and looked like a smaller rusted cousin of the Monopoly man. I could barely understand him. English was not his first language.

"I work in the basement," he said, pausing to search for words. "Her heart is not to scale."

Toby opened her eyes once and, seeing the man, flicked him off the sheets like a fly.

"In the morning," she said, "the bra goes back on."

But I was gone before she woke up a second time.

The Ear

The two professors sat in the cafeteria near a large bank of windows that afforded a view of the college's swimming pool one story below. It was a hot day and a few women sat on the edge of the pool with their backs to the men above who watched unashamedly, eating gyros and fries. They were talking about a documentary the young professor had seen the night before about secret collections in museums, halls of hermaphroditic statues and assorted Gnostica, until the young man lost his train of thought and stared quietly for some time. Realizing his young friend was not present, the older colleague spoke.

"What is it?" the old man asked.

"Nothing," the young man said. "It's just. My God. That woman has a beautiful figure."

The old man looked down. There below them a new woman had emerged from the water. She lifted herself up with a twist of her torso so she too now sat with her back to them and spoke with her friends who were all resting between laps. She wore a bikini like the others, but hers was red and white striped. When she sat, she reclined in a classical pose with a strand of dark hair curled around her shoulder. It seemed to the young professor, the very outline of her shape was a keyhole through which one viewed the beauties of renaissance paintings.

"I am not saying this out of any sexual feelings for

her," the young man said, "but as an advocate of beauty, I'd like to go down there and tell her how beautiful she is. But that would be wrong. She wouldn't hear it right, I suppose."

"No," the old professor said. "She wouldn't."

"And still it's odd. I cannot look away." He stood up. "I may go down there."

Just as he was about to leave, the old professor spoke. "There is something freakish about beauty like that," the old man said, putting a hand up as if to stop him. He smiled, returned to his sandwich.

"What?" asked the young man, hesitating. "Do you know her?"

"I had her in a class once."

"And?"

"I happened to notice that she has an ear in the small of her back."

"An ear?" the young man said, fixing his eyes back on the old professor's pallid face.

"Yes."

"Are you sure? Her skin looks flawless from here."

"It's very small," the old man said. "She leaned over once and I saw it. It had a lobe and everything. She wore a small diamond stud in it even."

"An ear?"

"And an earring," the old man said.

The young professor looked down again at the woman on the edge of the pool and watched as she dove back into the water and ducked under a knotted lane rope to resume her laps.

"Why would she have an extra ear?" the young professor asked not so much to the old man but, perhaps, to the universe itself.

The old man put down his sandwich and, as a favor,

told the young man what he knew about beautiful women.

"All beautiful women have them," he said. "It's just they go unnoticed. Hers isn't an ear for normal hearing, you see. She has two fine ears already for that purpose. This ear is to hear what isn't being said. It is an ear that demands a truth that cannot be articulated easily. It cherishes the language of stillness. It longs for the art of the pause."

The old man took one long draught of his water, nodded, and excused himself to the restroom, leaving the young man alone, staring but not seeing the scene below him in a space voided of time. What awoke him finally from this reverie was the sight of the old man down below walking by the pool and holding the beautiful woman's red towel out from his body like the wingspan of a phoenix, just as she finished her final stroke in the pool.

If he had been a lip reader, the young man might have learned what the old man said to her to get her to lift herself toward him and turn so he could throw the towel over her soft curves. But the young professor was not looking at the old man's lips. Instead, his gaze remained fixed on the woman's back, searching frantically for the hidden ear before the old man draped the towel over her shoulders and she turned to walk with him side by side.

A Note of Thanks

They say the hardest thing to do is to make something from nothing, so many thanks to Heather Momyer for reaching out into the ether and bringing this book into the world. To Alban Fischer for the kick-ass cover, and to all the good people involved with Arc Pair Press for their assistance. To all the editors of the literary magazines these stories appeared in, thanks for taking the risk, in particular Jordan Bass, Philip Graham, Chris Chambers, Marthe Reed, and Bradford Morrow. For any people who read and gave me feedback on these stories over the years, thanks for not pouncing on the soft white underbelly of my fiction: Mike Jauchen, Kurt Wilt, and the actual Brian Sullivan, in particular. To my teachers, thanks for helping me figure out what I could do and how to do it better: Reggie Young, Ernest Gaines, Wendell Mayo, Tony Doerr, Chris Grimes, Dayana Stetco, and Rikki Ducornet. To my friend Wiley Cash for lighting the way and for shining more light on these stories. To my family near and far, to my friends and colleagues, I am grateful for your support. To Charlie, Genevieve, and Jude for filling my days with love and sometimes farts and barf, but mostly love. Lastly to Anna for loving me off the page and keeping me honest on it.

About the Author

Patrick Crerand lives with his wife and three kids in Dade City, Florida. He writes fiction and essays which have appeared in *McSweeney's Quarterly Concern*, *Conjunctions*, *New Orleans Review*, *Ninth Letter*, *Indiana Review*, *Cimarron Review* among others and have received special mention in *The Best American Nonrequired Reading* and *Best American Fantasy* anthologies. Currently, he is an Associate Professor of English Literature and Creative Writing at Saint Leo University in Florida, where he also teaches in the Low-Residency MA program.

Made in the USA
Monee, IL
29 December 2021

87541728R00042